Super Duper Pee Wee!

Super Duper Pee Wee!

JUDY DELTON

Illustrated by Alan Tiegreen

A YEARLING BOOK

Published by
Bantam Doubleday Dell Books for Young Readers
a division of
Bantam Doubleday Dell Publishing Group, Inc.
1540 Broadway
New York, New York 10036

ISBN: 0-440-40992-6

Printed in the United States of America

July 1995

10 9 8 7 6 5 4

For Olivia, my favorite granddaughter

Contents

CHAPTER 1

New Badge News

"The new badge we are going to earn," said Mrs. Peters, "is one of my favorites! It is the letter-writing badge!"

Mrs. Peters was the Pee Wee Scout leader of Troop 23. The troop met every Tuesday in her basement.

She waited to hear her Pee Wees cheer. She waited until they looked happy about their new badge. But they didn't. They began to groan.

"It sounds like school to me," said Molly

Duff to her best friend, Mary Beth Kelly. This was the first time Mrs. Peters had let Molly down. All the time she'd been a Pee Wee the badges had been exciting. Like the badge for skiing. Or fishing. Even baseball. Molly had nothing against letter writing— she liked to write to her grandma and her friends who moved away. But badges were for something special.

"It sounds like work, not like fun. Pee Wees are supposed to be fun," said Tim Noon.

"Just wait till I tell you about it!" said Mrs. Peters. "We are going to have a pen pal club! We will write to a group of children miles away. They live in a town out west called Golden Grove and are Pee Wees too, with a different leader. They are super duper troopers, and they can't wait to earn this badge along with us and become our new friends. Letter writing is a wonderful way to get to know new people and learn new things."

The word *learn* was not a word the Pee Wees wanted to hear. It was too much like studying in school.

"We've got friends," muttered Sonny Stone. Sonny was a mama's boy. His mom had married the fire chief a while back, and Molly thought he would grow up if he had a dad. But so far he hadn't.

"Everyone can use more friends," said Mrs. Peters, frowning. She didn't look happy about the poor response to her favorite badge.

Rachel Meyers was waving her hand. "I already have a pen pal, Mrs. Peters. She lives in Germany. She sent me her picture."

You might know Rachel would already have a pen pal, thought Molly. She always knew everything before the other Pee Wees. And her pen pal was not even in this country! She was all the way across the ocean, in Germany!

"Someday I'm going to Germany to visit her," Rachel went on. "As soon as I can speak German."

Mrs. Peters's new badge was not going over big, thought Molly. Some of the Pee Wees were crawling under the table, and some were yawning. This had never happened before! What if the Pee Wees rebelled! Her dad had told her about workers who didn't like things in the office and went on strike! Were the Pee Wees going to strike?

"That's very good, Rachel," said Mrs. Peters above the scuffle. "We won't have pen pals in Europe, but since you've had experience, you can help us with our project."

Another word like *learn*. *Project*. Projects were even more work than learning!

"We are going to learn to write a proper letter and then write to them and wait to

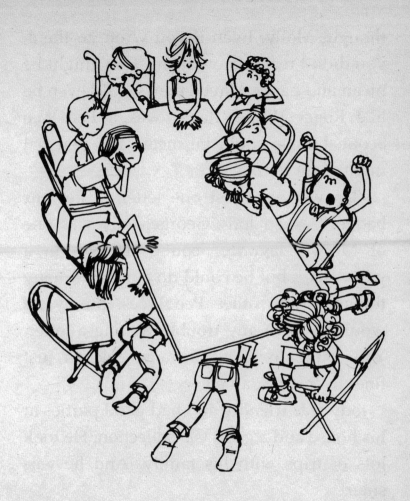

hear back. And maybe someday we will even get to meet our pen pals in person."

Who wanted to meet perfect strangers,

thought Molly. Even if you wrote to them, you didn't really know them. They might be mean and nasty. Maybe they would even be like Roger White. Roger was a Pee Wee Scout, but he could be mean. His pen pal might hate him!

"Do we write just one letter to get our badge?" asked Jody George. Jody was one of Molly's favorite Scouts. He was in a wheelchair, but he could do almost as many things as the other Pee Wees. Surely he wouldn't have any trouble writing a letter. You could do that from a wheelchair just fine. Even from a bed.

Jody was friendly and had good parties at his house and a good CD collection. He took lots of trips with his family. And he was smart.

"It's not the number of letters we write," Mrs. Peters said with a frown. "It would be nice to write back and forth to them and maybe write a few letters to other people.

Maybe one to your grandma if she is out of town and one to an author of your favorite books."

"My favorite author is dead," shouted Roger. "He's Mark Twain."

"Mine isn't," said Molly. "I'm going to write to Judy Delton. She wrote *Two Good Friends*. My mom used to read it to me when I was real little."

"I've got lots of her books," said Mary Beth.

"When you write to authors," said Mrs. Peters, "be sure to enclose a stamped envelope with your address on it, if you want a reply.

"But today," she went on, trying to get back to her subject, "what we need to do is learn how to write a good letter."

"Can we write a postcard?" asked Tracy Barnes.

"Can I call my pen pal on the phone, instead of writing?" asked Tim.

"I can fax a letter in my dad's office," said Patty Baker.

Molly thought Mrs. Peters looked sad.

"No postcards," she said firmly. "When you are on a vacation and want to send a picture postcard, that is fine. But we will start with letters. No phone calls. No faxes. We are going to write real old-fashioned letters, with stamps on them, like people used to send before there were shortcuts."

"That's called 'snail mail,'" said Lisa Ronning. "It's really slow."

"We are not in a hurry," said Mrs. Peters.

"Can we use a computer?" asked Ashley Baker. "My family does everything on the computer."

"Everything?" yelled Roger. "Ha, do you eat and sleep on it?"

"Do you bake bread in it?" said Sonny. He and Roger looked at each other and laughed.

Ashley ignored the boys.

"A personal letter should be handwritten," said their leader. "It is a chance to write neatly and in your best writing."

The Pee Wee Scouts were not crawling under the table now.

And they were not scuffling and talking.

They were not being super duper troopers.

Tim was making snoring noises, and two of the other boys were asleep.

Tracy was doing a crossword puzzle in a book her aunt had given her.

"What is a three-letter word for pine tree?" she whispered to Molly.

Roger was reading his joke book.

Mrs. Peters's latest project was definitely not off to a good start.

CHAPTER 2

Roger Gets a Girl

"Do you know what?" asked Sonny. "My aunt belongs to a pen pal club. It's a club where you meet someone to marry. She gets pictures of all these guys and she decides who she likes and writes to them."

Now everyone was awake.

"Do we have to marry our pen pal?" asked Lisa. "My mom wouldn't like that."

Molly did not want to marry a pen pal. She was going to marry Kevin Moe. He was a Pee Wee too. She liked Kevin. He was going to be mayor of their town when he grew up.

"You guys can't marry your pen pal," Jody said, laughing, from his wheelchair. "You aren't even old enough."

"Jody is right," said Mrs. Peters, looking impatient. Their leader hardly ever got impatient. "You do not need to marry your pen pal, now or ever." She glared at Sonny.

"What if we want to write to more than one pen pal?" asked Ashley. "Do we get one badge for every pen pal?"

"Just one badge," said Mrs. Peters. "And one pen pal. I think most of you will find one correspondent is enough. Plus your grandma or a friend."

"What's 'correspondent'?" whispered Tim to Tracy.

"I think it's like a secret agent," she answered. "Or a spy."

"Hey, I'd like to write to a spy!" said Roger.

"I don't want to be a spy!" cried Sonny. "Mrs. Peters, do I have to spy?"

"A correspondent isn't a spy," scoffed Ashley. "It's someone you write to."

Mrs. Peters turned and wrote a sample letter on a green slate. She held it up.

"Up here," she said, pointing to the right-hand corner of the letter, "you write your own address. And under it, you write the date."

Mrs. Peters went on, "On the left side, you put the name and address of the person you are writing to."

"I don't do all that stuff when I write to my grandma," said Patty Baker, who was Kenny's twin. "I just say 'Dear Grandma' right away."

"That's fine," said their leader. "But we want to learn the right way. We do not know our pen pals like we know our grandmas."

"That is a business-letter form," said Ashley.

"Now," Mrs. Peters said, "we start our letter right here at the left margin. We write 'Dear Grandma' or 'Dear Ronald,' and then we indent and begin what we want to say."

"What's 'indent'?" shouted Sonny.

"It's when you make something new, like indenting the telephone," said Tim.

The Pee Wees burst into laughter.

"That's 'invent,' dummy," said Roger.

Mrs. Peters held up her hand for silence. "You go in three spaces to start your news, just like you do when you write a story in school."

She pointed to the letter.

It was indented.

It said,

Dear Grandma,

How are you? I hope you are having good weather. I hope you come and see us soon. How is grandpa?

Love, Jane.

"Who is Jane?" shouted Tim.

"She's a made-up person," said Ashley in disgust. "This is a sample letter."

"It's boring," said Lisa. "I wouldn't write such a boring letter as that."

Mrs. Peters laughed.

"You're right," she said. "It is up to you all to write much more interesting letters! Letters that tell what you are doing and what you think about and how you feel about things."

Molly began to get excited. She liked to write stories. And she liked new friends. This would be both of those things.

Mrs. Peters talked about nice handwriting.

She talked about no holes in the paper from erasing.

She talked about clear addresses on envelopes that the mail carriers could read with or without their glasses.

And then she held up a basket.

"In this basket are names and addresses of our pen pals. Each one of you will draw a name. He or she will be your new pen pal and friend."

The Pee Wees drew names one at a time.

"Hey, mine's a girl!" said Roger. "I don't want to write to a girl!"

"We are all people, Roger," said their leader. "These Scouts are all people and have many of the same interests and hobbies as you do. You will find things you have in common when you write to them."

"I'm sorry for that poor girl who has Roger for a pen pal," said Rachel.

Molly hoped she had drawn a girl's name. Mrs. Peters said boys and girls were both people, but sometimes Roger and Sonny acted like the girls weren't quite there. Like perhaps the boys had a little more growing up to do first.

Molly put her new pen pal's name in her pocket. She would wait till she was in her

room at home to see who it was. She liked to do things like this alone in the privacy of her room, not in front of everyone.

The Pee Wees told good deeds they'd done and sang their song and said their pledge. Then the meeting was over, and

Molly ran ahead of the others on the way home. She had the name of her pen pal in her pocket. What if that pen pal was a boy? Or rather, what if he was a boy like Roger?

CHAPTER 3

No Trading Pen Pals

"**W**hat's new at Scouts?" called Molly's dad as she rushed through the house to her room.

"We're getting another badge," she called from the stairs.

In her room Molly sat on the edge of her bed, even though her mother said it would ruin the mattress. She opened the little folded piece of paper she'd drawn out of the basket. Her pen pal's name and address were typed. Some of the letters were written over as if mistakes had been made. But the name looked clear. It said, "Lyle Kester, 62 South Main Street." Her pen pal was a boy.

"Rat's knees!" said Molly. She stood up and stamped her foot on the floor so hard her dad called up to her, "Don't knock the house down, Molly!"

"My pen pal is a boy," she called down to her dad from the top of the stairs.

She walked down the steps and told her dad about the badge. "I don't want to write to a boy," she said sadly.

"What's the matter with a boy?" asked her dad. "I'm a boy, and you like me!"

Molly laughed. "You're not a boy," she said. "You're a man."

Her dad looked at the slip of paper in Molly's hand.

"Well, I was a boy once," he said. "And Lyle will be a man like me someday."

Molly frowned. "He might not be like you," she said. "He might be like Roger."

"Horrors!" said Mr. Duff, pretending to be shocked.

But he did have to admit it was true. He could be like Roger. No one knew yet what kind of a boy Lyle was. "It's a fifty-fifty chance you have," he said. "Roger or me."

Molly's mother came home and heard the story.

"I'm sure Lyle will be a very nice boy," she said.

Molly wanted to believe her, but after all, she didn't know any more about Lyle than Molly did.

After supper Molly fed her dog, Skippy, and went up to her room to write a letter. After the meeting she couldn't wait to write to her pen pal. She wanted to be the first one to write and the first one to get an answer. But now she wasn't as eager.

The phone rang. It was Mary Beth. She

said, "My pen pal's name is Shari, with an *i*."

Mary Beth's pen pal was definitely a girl. Mary Beth was always lucky.

"Rachel got someone named Heather. And Ashley got a boy!"

"So did I," said Molly.

Mary Beth didn't say anything for a minute. Then she said, "I wouldn't mind having a boy to write to. I mean, it could be kind of romantic. Or else it could be like having a brother or a cousin."

The cousin or brother sounded okay. But Molly scoffed at romantic. "I'm going to marry Kevin. Or maybe Jody."

"You never know," said Mary Beth. "My brother's friend married a girl he wrote to when he was in the army."

Molly sighed. This wasn't solving the pen pal problem.

Then she thought of something. "Let's trade," she said. "I'll trade you Lyle for Shari."

Mary Beth was quiet again. She's thinking of an excuse, thought Molly.

"I would, but I don't think Mrs. Peters would like it," said Mary Beth.

"Pooh, she wouldn't even know," said Molly.

"Still, I think it's against the rules."

"What rules?" asked Molly.

"Pee Wee rules," said Mary Beth.

Molly had never heard of a Scout rule that said you could not exchange pen pals. Come to think about it, she had never heard of any Pee Wee rules, period.

"It would be kind of like cheating," said Mary Beth. "I mean, that's the point of drawing a name. The name we draw is the one we are supposed to write to."

Mary Beth changed the subject and began to talk about a party her sister was having.

After Molly hung up, Tracy called to talk about pen pals. Hers was a girl.

"I'm glad I didn't get a boy," she said. "I mean, I like boys and everything, but what if he was like Roger?"

"I know," said Molly.

She hung up and hoped no one else would call her. She sat at her desk and took out a piece of paper with a big *M* on it. The *M* had flowers winding through it and down the side of the paper. What would

Lyle's paper have on it? she wondered. It wouldn't have flowers crawling around a big *L*, she knew. In fact, it wouldn't even have an *L* on it. If it had anything, it would have a spaceship or race car. And if he was like Roger, he'd probably write on an old candy wrapper or a paper towel.

Suddenly Molly caught herself. This was not fair. Jody would not write on a candy wrapper or towel. Neither would Kevin. This was what her mother called "discrimination." Mrs. Peters had said they were all people. Molly had to be careful. She neatly wrote her address at the top of the paper, with the date. Then she wrote Lyle's name and address on the other side, across from it. She left a little space and wrote, "Dear Lyle."

Here she had to stop to think. Finally she indented and wrote, "I drew your name from a basket. So you are my pen pal. I mean, if you write back you are. My name is Molly and I'm seven. How old are you? Do you have a dog? I do. Mrs. Peters is our leader. We go on trips and do good deeds and get badges. I have a mother and father and no brothers or sisters. I have lots of friends in Pee Wee Scouts. My best friend is Mary Beth. Her pen pal is a girl. Mine isn't. My other friends are Jody and Kevin. They are boys, but they are nice anyway."

Molly read this much over and erased the last line. It might make Lyle feel bad. Then she wrote, "Some of the boys in our troop are mean. Especially one named Roger. I hope you aren't like him."

She read it over and erased it. It was even worse than the other sentence!

In its place she wrote, "Love, Molly Duff."

But did she love Lyle? She didn't even know him! She crossed out love and wrote,

"Yours truly." Then she folded it in half and put it in an envelope. The envelope had an *M* with flowers just like the stationery.

Molly was worn out. Letter writing took a lot of thinking and it made her fingers stiff.

She went downstairs and asked her mother for a stamp. She'd mail it tomorrow. Then all she had to do was sit and wait for a letter back. It didn't really matter if Lyle was nice or not. Even if he wrote only one letter, she'd get her badge.

CHAPTER 4

From Whole Room to Half a Room

The next morning Molly mailed the letter to Lyle. Mary Beth mailed her pen pal letter too.

"I don't know what to say in a letter," whined Sonny when the girls met him in the park riding his bike. "And I can't spell all those words."

"Use a dictionary," said Mary Beth.

Sonny sighed, as if a dictionary was definitely too hard.

"I can't read dictionaries," he said. "I can't read those hard words."

Sonny was lazy, thought Molly. He only wanted to do things that were really easy. It was his mother's fault. She treated him like a baby instead of a seven-year-old.

Sonny rode off and the girls sat on a bench in the warm sun watching the robins dig for worms.

"This is an easy badge to earn," said Mary Beth. "Writing a letter is simple. I'm going to write a bunch of letters to people I know."

"What if our pen pals don't write back?" said Molly.

"They will," said Mary Beth. "They have to. Or they won't get their badge." She stood up and stretched. "I have to go home and baby-sit my little brother now," she added.

Molly wished she had brothers and sis-

ters. Everyone else did, it seemed, but her. Her family was too small.

But when she got home, her mother had some news that looked as if it might change all that.

"Auntie Ree is coming to live with us for a while," she said, hanging up the phone.

Auntie Ree was her mother's sister. Her name was Marie, but when Molly was little she couldn't say "Marie" so she called her "Auntie Ree." Auntie Ree was married and lived in a fine house of her own. Molly could understand her coming to visit. But her mother did not say visit. She said "live."

"Is Uncle Chuck coming too?" asked Molly, thinking how quickly her wish for a bigger family had been granted.

"They are getting a divorce," she said. She looked sad. "They have been separated, but I hoped they would get back together. Instead, they are divorcing."

This was not happy news. This was not news that Molly would be getting a new sister or brother. A divorced aunt was not the way to add to a too-small family.

"You may have to share your room for a while," said her mother. "Till we see how long she will be here. The den is all torn up, and the couch is gone to be re-covered."

She put her arms around Molly and said, "Do you mind very much? I know it won't be easy." Molly did mind. But she did not want to make her mother even sadder.

"No," she said. "I don't mind."

But she did!

Her own darling little room! The place where she went to be alone when she was sad or happy or just to read a good book!

Her other twin bed was where her stuffed animals sat. It was where Mary Beth slept when she stayed overnight and they talked long into the night and told ghost stories and secrets. It was where they had sleep overs. Did they want her Auntie Ree at a sleep over? Especially if she was crying all over the place?

But it was true about the den being torn up. Her dad had begun to re-paper the walls and had not had time to finish.

She wondered if it was a lie to tell her mother she didn't mind. Or if it was one of those little white lies it was okay to tell to be polite, when it would be rude to tell the truth.

"When is she coming?" asked Molly.

"Tomorrow," said her mom. She wiped her eyes and blew her nose. "We have a lot of work to do before she comes. Will you mind if we make some room for her things?"

Molly shook her head and went upstairs with her mother.

"We'll have to clear some drawers in your dresser for Marie," she said.

Molly helped her mother put her sweaters with her underwear. She put her socks with her hair ribbons and pajamas. It looked crowded and it looked messy. But it was for a good cause. She liked her aunt.

"Maybe she will make up with Uncle

Chuck," said Molly. "Maybe she will miss him and go home."

Molly's mother sniffled. That was the wrong thing to say.

Her mother shook her head. "A divorce means it's over," she said. "They are selling the house."

Poor Auntie Ree! Put out of her nice house to come and live in a bedroom! And not even a whole bedroom at that! A half of a bedroom. A half of a closet. And half of a dresser! Could Uncle Chuck be that bad?

This morning when Molly had gone out to mail her letter, she had had a whole room of her own and a happy life. She had come home an hour later, and now she had a half a room and no secrets and a life that looked like it might not be happy.

That's what she got for wanting a bigger family! Once, her teacher had told the class to be careful what they wished for. Well, she hadn't! And now she had a bigger family.

Molly's mother took her pretty dotted swiss curtains down and washed them. She vacuumed the rug and Molly dusted. Her mother put clean towels out and her dad fixed the switch on the bed lamp.

"Be good to Auntie Ree," he said, patting Molly on the head.

What did he mean, be good? Did he mean smile at her? Wait on her? Take her to the Dairy Princess? Find her a new husband?

Molly wanted to go to her room and cry. But her room wasn't hers anymore. And no one wanted any more tears.

CHAPTER 5

Auntie Ree Moves In

Supper was a quiet meal. And there was no dessert. Molly's mother said she wondered what Marie would like to eat.

"I'll go to the market on the way home from work tomorrow," offered her dad. "I'll get something good."

Molly finished eating and went to her room. There didn't seem to be anything to do but go to bed. She crawled into her clean little bed, and as she fell asleep she smelled the lemon furniture polish her mother had used.

When she woke up in the morning her mother was putting a vase of tulips on the table between the two beds.

"I thought flowers would cheer Marie up," said Mrs. Duff.

If things were as bad as they felt, it would take a lot more than flowers to cheer her aunt, thought Molly.

Molly got dressed and ate breakfast and went out to play with Tracy and Lisa and Patty. She didn't tell them about sharing her room. They talked about pen pals. They had all mailed their letters. When she got home, her aunt was there.

She gave Molly a big hug and said, "Why, just look how you've grown!"

She didn't look sad, thought Molly. Not as sad as her mother. Maybe she was glad to be there.

In Molly's room, Marie's things were all over the place. One suitcase was on the bed, spilling with jeans and shirts and jewelry. Her makeup was on Molly's dresser, and in the bathroom were her hair dryer, panty hose, and her bathrobe. On the dining room table was her tennis racket.

Auntie Ree had moved in.

"Chuck is sending on some more of my things," said Marie. "I couldn't take everything on the plane."

Molly wondered where any more things would go!

"Here, this is for you!" said her aunt, handing Molly a big box with pink tissue paper and a big white bow.

Did divorced people go out shopping for presents? Maybe it was like a party. A divorce party instead of a wedding party!

"I don't know if you'll like it or not," chattered her aunt as Molly opened the box.

She pulled out a big stuffed Scottie dog
with a wide red ribbon around his neck.

"I hope you aren't too old for stuffed animals," said Marie.

"I love them," said Molly.

It was nice of her aunt to bring her a gift.

"No one is ever too old for stuffed animals," said Mrs. Duff. "Molly keeps them on her bed."

Molly hugged the big soft dog. "He's like Skippy!" she said. "Except he's black." She ran over and gave her aunt a hug too. "Thank you," she said. "I think I'll name him Harry."

"It's a good name," her aunt said, laughing. "He has a lot of long hair."

Her mother had a package too. It was a pretty teapot in the shape of a strawberry. It even had a green leaf on the top of it.

"That's for us to have a tea party some afternoon," said Marie.

When Molly's dad came home, they all ate dinner, and it was a cheerier meal than the one the night before. Mr. Duff even poured three glasses of wine.

After Marie had gone to her room to unpack some more, Molly helped her mother do the dishes. "Auntie Ree doesn't seem too sad," she said.

"Well," said her mother, "she was always the plucky one in the family. She doesn't believe in feeling sorry for herself."

The next afternoon, Molly's aunt took her and Mary Beth to the zoo and then out for ice cream. It was fun getting to know her aunt better. When they got home, two men were delivering some exercise equipment.

"I thought I could put it in the basement," said Marie. "I have to get back in shape, you know!"

Her aunt looked in good shape the way she was, thought Molly. On Sunday her aunt got a newspaper and read the want ads.

"It's time I stopped vacationing and got a job," she said, running her finger down the list. "Here is someone looking for a fry cook. And a nurse in a doctor's office. But I think I'd like to work in a bookstore."

A job? If she was looking for a job, Auntie Ree must be planning on staying! Exercise equipment was one thing. But a job was something you went to every day, maybe for the rest of your life! Molly might never get her room back! She'd never be able to have another overnight party the rest of her life!

And her aunt snored. Sometimes it kept Molly awake and she was too tired to get up in the morning.

But her mother seemed to enjoy having her sister there. Instead of making her sad, she seemed to cheer her up! And her aunt did take Molly shopping, and she showed her how to play tennis. Molly felt guilty wanting her to leave. Auntie Ree seemed to enjoy being with Molly. It felt more and more like being with a friend.

"It's just that our house is too small!" Molly told Mary Beth one afternoon when they were cutting out paper doils on the Kellys' front porch.

"She needs a home of her own," said Mary Beth. "And a new husband. I think she's ready to date."

Molly was shocked. She felt bad about her uncle Chuck. How could Mary Beth want her aunt to go out with someone else?

"That's what you do when you're divorced," said Mary Beth. "You find someone new."

"She doesn't even know anybody here," said Molly.

"Well, then it's up to us to find her someone," said her friend. "Let's make a list of who we know."

Mary Beth ran and got a piece of paper and a pencil.

She wrote down, "Mr. Stenstrom."

"Who is he?" asked Molly.

"The butcher at the market," said Mary

Beth. "My mom says he's looking for a wife."

Mary Beth frowned. "He is bald, though," she said. "He may be too old for your aunt." She crossed his name off.

"I can't think of anyone who isn't bald," she said.

"Well, there's always Roger's father," said Molly. "He isn't bald."

"You'd be Roger's cousin!" shouted Mary Beth. "If they got married, you'd be *related* to Roger! And your aunt would be Roger's *mother*!"

Molly tried to picture Roger in her own little house on holidays. She might need brothers and cousins but she didn't need Roger! That was definitely a bad plan! Roger at her house on Christmas Eve, Roger there pushing and shoving on her birthday!

"Still," said Mary Beth, "you can't be self-ish. We have to do what's good for your aunt. Even though you like her, it's definitely not good for her to live with you forever."

Molly thought about what it would be like to share her bedroom with her aunt when Molly was a teenager. And then she thought about Roger for a cousin. It was a hard choice.

But Mary Beth was right. She couldn't be selfish. She wanted her aunt to be happy. And she did want her bedroom back.

Molly sighed. "I guess Mr. White would be a good husband. He is nicer than Roger."

"And he has more hair than Mr. Stenstrom," said Mary Beth sensibly.

Molly sighed. She had lots of things to worry about. She had a boy for a pen pal, and he had not written to her yet. And she had to get her badge. The other Scouts were getting letters. And now she had to find a husband for Auntie Ree.

When she got home, she found out her worries had just begun.

CHAPTER 6

Pillow Fight

When Molly turned into her yard, she knew something was not right. The front door was standing open, and it was always closed. She could hear loud voices from inside, and no one in her family ever talked that loudly. And it was almost dinnertime, but there was no smell of anything cooking from the kitchen.

Her parents did not hear her come in. They were standing in the living room talking, but the talking wasn't friendly. It was angry.

Molly heard her father say, "I don't care if you do!"

Do what? Molly wondered.

Then her mother called him a stubborn mule, and her father said, "Well, if that is the way you feel . . ." and then Molly's mother did something Molly had never seen her do. She threw something at Molly's dad. It was only a pillow from the couch, but she threw it hard and it hit Molly's dad in the chest. He looked surprised and turned and walked out of the room. Her mother's hair was hanging in her face, and her face was red.

In a minute Mrs. Duff walked into the kitchen and started getting dinner. Pots and pans banged onto the stove. Silverware clattered. Usually when her mother cooked she was very quiet. The only noise she made was to hum a song or put something in the blender.

Molly ran up to her room to be alone, and for a change her aunt was not there. She threw herself onto her bed, shaking with fear. What had gone wrong? Was it something she had done? Had Molly caused her parents to fight?

Molly knew that other families fought sometimes, but hers never did!

And she knew that parents who fought often got a divorce! Were her mother and father going to get a divorce too? Was divorce contagious, like the flu or a sore throat? Had they caught it from Auntie Ree?

Now Molly's stomach began to ache, and she felt shaky all over. What would happen if her father moved into another house? Where would Molly live?

Or what if her mother threw something bigger and heavier than a pillow? On TV Molly had seen parents throw books and vases and dishes and even things made out of metal. This could happen next, and it could be all her fault. Molly put her face into her pillow and began to sob. She fell asleep crying, and when her mother called her to dinner she woke up with the same awful feeling inside of her. She hoped that it had been a dream, but she knew it wasn't.

Her mother had combed her hair and her dad was in his regular place at the table. Were her mother and father being brave, like Auntie Ree? Was this whole family a brave family, except her? She didn't feel brave, she felt scared.

Auntie Ree came in with a cake from the bakery for dessert. "I found a job!" she said. "This cake is to celebrate!"

Auntie Ree talked and talked about her new job, which was at an insurance agency instead of a bookstore, and her parents acted interested and polite, but they were quieter than usual. Molly wondered if she had imagined the fight. Or made it worse than it was. People who were getting a divorce did not sit at the table together politely, eating bratwurst on buns, no matter how brave they were. Did they?

After dinner her dad cleared the table and put an apron on and washed the dishes.

Auntie Ree dried them, and Molly put them away. It all looked normal.

But Molly wasn't fooled. Her parents had fought. Something was the matter. Molly knew people called lawyers to get divorces, and her mother was on the telephone right now!

"We'll have to go shopping, you and I," said her aunt to Molly. "I'll need some new clothes for my job, and you can help me pick them out."

Molly nodded. How could her aunt think of new clothes now, when her sister was about to leave her husband and small daughter? What kind of a family was this, with everyone in it getting divorced?

That night in bed, Molly thought of telling Auntie Ree the whole story and asking her if it was true. And she thought of asking her mother face to face.

But she couldn't talk about it. Maybe because she wasn't sure she wanted to hear the answer. What if they said she was right, they were getting a divorce? No, it was better this way. There was a chance she was wrong.

The next day, the Pee Wee Scouts met, and Molly decided she would take Mary Beth aside and confide the awful news to her. But she was not alone with her, and she did not want Rachel and Ashley and Roger and Sonny to know about her personal problems. Besides, Mary Beth had a letter from her pen pal, Shari, and was dying to read it to her.

"Shari has lots of brothers and sisters too!" said Mary Beth. "And she likes animals just like I do. And look at this stamp. I'm going to collect the stamps. My dad's getting me a stamp album."

Molly decided to put her problem out of her mind during the Scout meeting, but it always seemed to be there, even when the others read the letters they got from their pen pals. What fun were pen pals now? What she needed were parents who were pals.

"Mrs. Peters, Mrs. Peters," called Ashley. "Can I read the letter I got from Jason?"

"Yes," said their leader. "And what a good response we have already! So many of you wrote and got answers right away!"

" 'Dear Ashley,' " read Ashley. " 'I like horses too. I've got a horse named Flash. He likes radishes. If you come to visit me, I will let you ride Flash. Sometimes I fall off when he jumps the fence. If you fall off, it's okay. The ground is soft because mud is soft, and it's all mud now. Yours sincerely, Jason.' "

The Pee Wees all laughed about the mud. Roger fell off his chair into pretend mud and walked around the room shaking it off his arms and legs.

Mary Beth read her letter from Shari, and Rachel read her letter from Heather.

"My letter is real long," said Rachel. All the Pee Wees looked over her shoulder as she read.

" 'My dad is a medical person too,' " read Rachel. " 'He is an M.D., a medical doctor.' "

Here Rachel stopped to say, "Isn't that a coincidence, Mrs. Peters? That the pen pal I got has a dad who's a doctor, and my dad is a dentist?"

"Yeah, yeah, you can pull teeth and operate on each other," said Roger. "Big deal."

Rachel looked at Roger in disgust. "You're just jealous," she said, "because you didn't get a letter back from your pen pal."

"Hey, I didn't even write to her yet," said Roger.

"Well, she won't write back, you can bet on that," said Rachel. "Once she finds out what a creep you are."

Rachel finished reading Heather's long letter.

Then Kevin and Jody each read their pen pal letters. They were collecting stamps too. Molly wondered if Jody's pen pal was in a wheelchair. She wished that Jody could be her pen pal. Or Kevin. But that would mean they would live far away in Golden Grove, and that would not be a good thing. It was better to have them right here in town.

Some of the Pee Wees had written to authors they liked and were waiting for letters. Tracy had written to her grandma and had a letter to read from her.

"My grandma plays bingo," said Tracy. "She won me a little TV for my room."

After the letters, the Pee Wees told good deeds and sang their song and said their pledge. Then they ate cupcakes decorated with make-believe postage stamps. Sonny's mother helped serve them.

On the way home Molly wanted to tell Mary Beth about her parents' argument, but

Mary Beth wanted to talk about plans to fix up Roger's father with her Auntie Ree.

Instead of finding Auntie Ree a husband, it might be her own *mother* who would need one, thought Molly. Auntie Ree seemed happy enough with her new job. She didn't act like she wanted a husband.

But that was not fair. As Mary Beth had said to her, Auntie Ree needed a husband and a home of her own. And Molly needed her room back. Just in case divorce really *was* catchy, it might be good to separate the sisters till this was all over.

CHAPTER **7**

Good Detective Work

The girls sat on their favorite park bench to plan Auntie Ree's first date.

"How can we get them to go on a date without knowing it's a date?" asked Molly. "I don't think my aunt will go if we tell her we found someone for her to marry."

Mary Beth nodded. "She probably doesn't know she needs to marry Mr. White," she said. "Roger's father probably doesn't know how happy he'll be married to Auntie Ree, either." She sighed. "Adults are so difficult," she said. "They never seem to see what's good for them."

"Well, we can't tell Roger," said Molly. "He doesn't even know he needs a mother."

"Maybe there will be some PTA meeting they can meet at," said Mary Beth.

"There are no PTA meetings when school is out," said Molly.

Mary Beth snapped her fingers. "I have it!" she said. "Your aunt can walk Skippy, and Mr. White can walk his dog, and they can meet and talk about the dogs! Then they can talk about other stuff like having children and where they'll live."

"Auntie Ree doesn't like dogs much," said Molly. "And Roger doesn't have a dog."

"We could get him one from the pound," said Mary Beth.

"Even if Mr. White has one, he might not

walk it," said Molly. "What if he has Roger walk it? We don't want my aunt to meet *Roger*! If she met him first, she'd never marry his dad!"

"So forget the dog," said Mary Beth grumpily. "It was just an idea."

"Where do they both go?" asked Molly. "At night after work?"

"The grocery store!" shouted Mary Beth. "Everyone gets groceries. Even Roger has to eat! They can run into each other at the market!"

"Rat's knees!" shouted Molly. "It's simple! Let's go over to Roger's house and ask him where his dad shops!"

"We can't just *ask* him," said Mary Beth. "We have to make it sound natural, kind of work it into the conversation so he won't be suspicious."

The girls ran home and got their bikes. Then they rode to Roger's house.

"What if he isn't home?" asked Molly.

"He's home," said Mary Beth. "Where would he be? He hasn't got many friends, he's so mean."

Mary Beth was right. When the girls got

near his house, they saw Roger carving something into the bark on a tree in his yard.

"What do you guys want?" he said suspiciously.

"We're just taking a bike ride," said Molly.

"Yeah, well ride someplace else."

"It's a public street," said Molly.

"We can do what we want," said Mary Beth. "And you're defacing that tree. It won't grow if you cut its bark."

"Did you come over here to tell me I can't carve my own tree?" said Roger.

"It isn't your tree," said Molly, stamping her foot. "Trees belong to everyone!"

"Not trees in my own yard," said Roger.

This wasn't going well, thought Molly. It was awfully hard not to fight with Roger.

"I think you should get some fertilizer for that tree," said Mary Beth. "You can get it at

64

the *grocery store* in the plant department. Your dad can get it when he shops."

"Get out of here," said Roger. "Leave me alone."

This was going to be harder than they figured, thought Molly. It was easy to see why Roger had so few friends. It was a wonder he wasn't thrown out of the Pee Wees. They'd have to try a nicer approach.

"Would you like to come on a bike ride with us?" she asked sweetly. "We could ride by the grocery store and stuff."

"Why would I want to ride with you guys?" Roger asked.

"Come down to the creek with us," said Mary Beth. "We can dig for some night crawlers and sell them."

Molly looked at her friend in surprise. Mary Beth hated worms! She was really going all out to get Roger on their side!

Roger looked like he had a lightbulb over

his head. "Ho *ho!*" he said. "I get it! You guys are trying to trick me into something!"

How could he know? thought Molly.

"Which one of you likes me?" Roger stood up with a big grin on his face. "Which one of you guys wants to be my girlfriend?"

So Roger didn't know about her aunt. He thought it was him they were after! If they said, "Not in your *dreams,* mister!" Roger would be mad again. If they said one of them did like him, he would spread it all over town that one of them wanted to be his girlfriend!

"We just want to be friends," said Mary Beth. "I mean, all three of us."

Roger stopped carving the tree and sat down on his front steps.

The girls sat down too. Roger didn't shove them off.

"It's hot out," said Mary Beth. "A good day for a barbecue."

"I might stop at the grocery store on the

way home and get some hot dogs," said Molly. "What is the closest grocery store around here, Roger?"

"What's all this grocery store stuff?" asked Roger. "We go to Maxwell's. Down on Main Street."

Molly took her little notebook from her jacket pocket and wrote down "Maxwell's. Main Street."

"And when do you shop?" asked Mary Beth.

"My dad gets stuff on his way home from work," said Roger. "He gets these great big steaks, this thick!"

Roger held his fingers apart about three inches and made loud chewing noises with his mouth.

Leave it to Roger to want to eat poor friendly cows, thought Molly.

"Every night?" said Mary Beth. "Does he stop and get steaks every night?"

Roger shrugged. "Some nights he gets a

great big fish," he said. Now Roger was casting an imaginary fish line out into the yard.

Mary Beth was getting impatient. She stood up with her hands on her hips and said, "What day and time does your dad go grocery shopping?"

"What's it to you?" shouted Roger, going into his house and slamming the screen door. "You guys are nuts, do you know that?"

The girls got on their bikes and rode toward home.

"Well, we know what store," said Mary Beth. "We'll just have to hang around and watch for his dad."

"But how are we going to get my aunt down there?" asked Molly.

"Sales!" said Mary Beth. "We'll clip coupons. Does your aunt like mushrooms? Room freshener?"

Molly sighed. Getting a husband for

Marie was so much work, she should get a badge for it!

Her problems were not going away.

Her aunt.

Her mother.

Her father.

Her pen pal.

Her badge.

When would something good happen?

When Molly got home, something did!

CHAPTER 8

Molly Gets a Letter

"You have some mail," said Auntie Ree when Molly got in the house.

Auntie Ree held up a letter. A fat one. It had Molly's name on it.

Molly took the letter and ran up to her room. The postmark on the envelope said Golden Grove! Her pen pal had written to her! She did have a pen pal after all! Even if it was a boy. She might get that badge after all.

Something smelled like lilacs. Molly

sniffed the air. It was coming from the envelope! Did Lyle use perfumed stationery?

Molly took her little letter opener from
her desk and slit the envelope. She unfolded
the big, thick letter. It was on several sheets
of notebook paper, and the handwriting
was big with lots of loops.

Dear Molly,

I got your letter. It took a long time
because it had the wrong name on the
envelope. My name is Kyle, and not
Lyle. I'm not a boy, but everyone thinks
I am because Kyle is a boy's name. Lyle
is too, I think. I was named after my
uncle. He's my godfather. There are no
boys in the family to be named after
him so it was just me or no one.

I'm glad you are my pen pal. I have a
dog too. What kind is yours? I don't
have any brothers or sisters either! Tell

me your favorite color and your favorite book.

My mom and dad are divorced. I live
with my mom. But I go stay with my
dad sometimes. He lives in California
and we go swimming in the ocean and
have picnics and ride horses. It's fun
having two homes. If I get bored in one
I can go to the other one!

I hope we can be friends and tell each
other secrets. Write back fast.

Love, Kyle.

Then she had a long row of *x*'s and *o*'s
across the bottom of the page.

Molly couldn't believe her eyes! Her pen
pal was a girl! She was an only child and
had a dog and she wanted to be Molly's
friend! It was too good to be true! And her
letter was *long*! Longer than Molly's. Longer
than even Heather's!

But the biggest surprise was that her parents were divorced and Kyle felt okay about it! Molly had never thought that something so awful could happen and you could still be a happy family and go to school and write to pen pals and have a dog.

Molly got out a sheet of school paper instead of her flowered stationery. She needed more room to write this time. She started writing and before long she had filled both sides of the paper. She told Kyle all about her friends and Skippy and her aunt and Mr. White and all about her worries that her parents could be getting a divorce too.

When she finished, she felt good. Very good. She had needed to tell someone all those things. And if Kyle liked having two homes better than one, maybe a divorce wasn't so bad. Molly hoped (if her parents did divorce) that her dad would move to California. The beach sounded like a lot of fun. Molly could take an airplane to see him and eat dinner out of those little trays way up high in the sky! Her dad would be waiting at the airport for her. She could see him now looking at the crowd for Molly, worrying that she might be lost. Then he would see her and get that big smile on his face and sweep her up into his arms, and she'd give him a big, big hug! He'd show her his new house and the city and the ocean. Maybe she could even meet Kyle and her dad.

And then when she was really lonely for home and her mother and the Pee Wees, she'd get on another plane and fly back to her own little room! Maybe Kyle even had two rooms of her own! One in each house.

Molly had been so lost in thought that she jumped when her father knocked at her door. She almost said, "I thought you were in California!" Molly had better get over this daydreaming. Her imagination had run away with her again. Her mother said she

had the wildest imagination of anyone she knew!

"Dinnertime!" said her dad. He didn't mention California.

After dinner Molly sealed the letter to

Kyle and went to the mailbox to mail it. She couldn't wait to get another letter back! Rat's knees, getting this badge was fun!

On Tuesday Molly read her letter from Kyle out loud at the Pee Wee Scout meeting. But if she and Kyle told secrets in their letters, she wouldn't read them out loud. They would be private. Molly would keep Kyle's letters in the fancy candy box from Valentine's Day. It was big and red and had a bow pasted right onto it. It was a perfect pen pal box.

Almost all the Pee Wees had a letter now.

Tim had a letter. And in the letter were two baseball cards.

"Hey, I think those guys are worth money!" said Kevin.

The Pee Wees looked envious of Tim. No one else got presents in their letters.

"I wonder why Tim got those," said Lisa. "Maybe he asked for them."

Molly shook her head.

"Tim is shy," she said. "He'd never do that."

"I'm so glad to see you are all enjoying getting this badge so much," said Mrs. Peters. "I knew it would be a fun badge to earn!"

Some of the Pee Wees groaned. They pretended it wasn't fun.

Mrs. Peters had a new map game to play. You had to draw cards to tell you how many spaces to move your little car. Whoever got to Golden Grove first, won. But some cards said, "Flat tire, go back three spaces" or "Detour six spaces." There were roadblocks and stop signs and "out of gas" stops.

"This is just like all those kid games, like Chutes and Ladders and Sorry! and Parcheesi," said Tracy.

"Yeah!" shouted Roger, moving his race car into Golden Grove. "I won!"

"You cheated!" shouted Ashley. "I saw you move when it was Tracy's turn!"

"He did," said Patty. "I saw him."

Molly noticed Rachel didn't have much to say.

Tim and Jody won the next games, and then it was time for cupcakes and good deeds and the pledge and song.

"Before long, we will get our badges!" said Mrs. Peters.

"Yeah!" shouted all the Pee Wees.

"Roger better hurry up and write a letter," said Patty.

On the way home, Mary Beth said, "I've got a plan for your aunt and Roger's dad."

Molly had been so excited about writing to Kyle that she had forgotten about Auntie Ree! But she did want her room back. Especially now that she would be writing private letters she didn't want anyone else to read. Her aunt might be looking for a pencil or a safety pin and pull open her drawer and find her candy box! Molly might write to Kyle about divorces and Roger's dad.

No, Auntie Ree couldn't stay forever. She was lucky to have Mary Beth for a friend. Mary Beth had a plan. And before long, Auntie Ree would be Mrs. White and in a home of her own!

CHAPTER 9

Grocery Store Stakeout

The girls sat down on Mary Beth's front steps.

"This is my plan," said Mary Beth. "I go down to Maxwell's and watch for Mr. White around suppertime. When he comes, I'll call you from their phone and you get your aunt down there as fast as you can."

"But what if my aunt won't come with me?" asked Molly.

Mary Beth waved her statement away with her hand. "Tell her it's an emergency," she said. "Tell her there's a fire you have to see, or you need a Popsicle right away. Now I'm going down there right now and hang out. You go home and wait for my call."

Mary Beth set off to the market, and Molly went home to wait. Her aunt came in, then her mom and dad.

"Are you busy tonight, Auntie Ree?" asked Molly.

"Nope," said her aunt. "Do you have something exciting for us to do?"

This was going to be easier than she thought! Molly *had* something exciting to do (what was more exciting than meeting the man she'd marry?), and her aunt was free and willing to go with her! Rat's knees, Mary Beth was smart!

"Maybe," said Molly. "I'm expecting a phone call."

"How mysterious," said Mr. Duff, setting the table.

Soon they all sat down to eat, but there was no phone call.

They finished their apple pie, and still no phone call.

They did the dishes and put them away and went in the living room to watch TV. Still there was no phone call.

Mr. Duff was dozing off in his chair when the phone rang.

But it was Rachel. "Heather wrote to me in purple ink!" she said. "And it smells like lilacs! I'm going to get some of that." Molly hung up.

Rat's knees! Here her aunt was ready to go, ready for a new husband, and nothing was happening.

"Was that the phone call you were waiting for?" asked Mrs. Duff.

Molly shook her head.

"Darn," said Auntie Ree. "No party tonight. And Mr. Right may have been there!"

Molly could not believe her ears! It was

almost as though her aunt was calling out for help! It was fate. It meant they were on the right track, all right. But where was Mr. White when they were ready?

When Molly was getting ready for bed, the call came.

"He didn't come," said Mary Beth, sighing. "I stood there at Maxwell's for ages. My mom was really mad I was late for supper."

"And we were all ready to come," said Molly. "Auntie Ree was waiting to meet Mr. Right."

"Well, he'll be there tomorrow night," said Mary Beth. "He has to shop, after all. Roger likes to eat."

The next evening, Mary Beth went back to the market. Molly waited for Auntie Ree to come home. But it got later and later and she didn't come.

"Where is Auntie Ree?" asked Molly at dinner. There were only three places set.

"She went to a movie with some people

from work," said Molly's mother. "I'm glad to see she's getting out and having a social life again."

The phone rang. It was Mary Beth. "Get down here!" she cried. "Mr. White is here in the produce section! He's picking out some melons, and he looks lonely!"

"My aunt's not home yet!" cried Molly.

Mary Beth sighed. "Well, I'll try to keep him here, but I'm not sure how long I can do it. Get down here the minute she comes home."

Molly hung up the phone and went to the living room to watch for her aunt. She looked down the street. She looked up the street. No sign of her.

"How long do movies last?" she asked her mother.

"Oh, a couple of hours, I guess," said her mom. "But they probably went out to eat first or stopped for a bite afterward."

Now Molly was cross. Mr. White couldn't

linger in the produce forever! Didn't her aunt know how hard it was to find the right man?

The phone rang. Molly answered it.

"What's taking so long?" asked Mary Beth. "Mr. White is in dairy products now and that's the last stop! His milk will get sour if he doesn't check out and get it home and into the fridge."

"She's not here yet," said Molly.

"I'll try to keep him here, but it won't be easy," said Mary Beth and hung up.

When she called again, she was angry. "I told him he was buying the wrong cereal, and I took him over and showed him the one with less fat and sugar, but he didn't buy it," said Mary Beth. "And he walked the other way when I tried to transfer his stuff into a better cart. I told him the wheels went the wrong way and they squeaked, but he just said, 'Who are you?' and walked to the checkout. I might be able to take the keys to his car, but I don't think my mom would like it."

"It's no use," said Molly. "Let him go."

"It's not your fault," Mary Beth said with a sigh. "We'll try again in a few days. Roger will eat all that food up fast."

But when the next chance came, neither of the girls was expecting it.

CHAPTER 10

Fate Steps In— and Out

On Saturday morning Auntie Ree took Molly and some of her Pee Wee friends to the mall.

"I want a new swimsuit," said Ashley.

"So do I!" said Auntie Ree. "Let's go in Sand and Surf and look at them!"

While they looked at swimsuits, the others sat on a bench in the mall and ate pretzels.

"Look!" shouted Mary Beth. She almost choked on a pretzel. "There are Roger and his dad!"

"Big deal," said Rachel in disgust. "I don't think Roger is anything to get excited about. Who wants to see him on a weekend when we don't have to?"

Something was bothering Rachel, thought Molly. She wondered what it was.

But Molly knew what Mary Beth meant! Fate had brought Marie and Mr. White inches apart!

"Get her!" hissed Mary Beth between her teeth. "Go in and get your aunt!"

Molly ran into the store. Her aunt was trying on a swimsuit.

"Come on out!" said Molly, dragging her by the hand. But Molly's aunt did not want to come out of the dressing room in the swimsuit.

"Look at the suit in the big mirror out here!" said Molly.

As her aunt stumbled out, Mary Beth was trying to talk Roger and his father into coming in the store and buying swimsuits.

Mr. White backed up. "Wait a minute, didn't I meet you in the market?" he said. "You were trying to sell me cereal! Now you want to sell me a swimsuit!"

"My mother says I'm a born salesperson," said Mary Beth.

"You're a born cuckoo!" shouted Roger. "Leave my dad alone!"

Now a small crowd was gathering, and Auntie Ree was back in her regular clothes, frowning at Molly.

"This is Molly's aunt Marie," said Mary Beth to Mr. White. "Marie, this is Mr. White."

In all the commotion, Molly did not think Mr. White and Auntie Ree even heard Mary Beth. But Mary Beth looked pleased with herself. "Now it's up to them," she whispered to Molly. "Our work is done."

The girls sat down on the bench to watch Aunt Marie fall in love with Mr. Right, who was Mr. White. But she didn't look like she was in love. No bells rang. No music played. Auntie Ree just said, "What is going on out here? I go in a shop and the next thing I know, you girls are creating a scene!"

"I don't need a swimsuit!" Mr. White was saying.

"Let my dad alone!" Roger was shouting. "Let's get out of here!"

"I hope Mrs. Peters doesn't hear about this," said Rachel. "It makes the Pee Wee Scouts look bad, causing scenes in the mall."

Rat's knees. How could love be a bad thing? If the Pee Wees let them alone, Mr. White and Auntie Ree could find out what they had in common. But now Roger was whining for a hot dog, and Auntie Ree was making sure none of the girls were lost.

"I wonder who that man was," said Auntie Ree as they moved on down the aisle. "He was rude!"

As Roger and his father walked away, Molly heard Roger's father asking him, "Who was that strange woman? And that girl tries to sell me something every time I meet her!"

"She's a Pee Wee Scout," muttered Roger. "I think she likes me."

"Oh, that's it!" said Mr. White, smiling. "Using me to get to you!"

When Molly and Mary Beth were alone, Mary Beth said, "I can't figure out what went wrong. We had them in the palm of our hand. Why didn't they fall in love?"

"Or at least go out on a date," muttered Molly.

It looked like Molly would have a roommate for a long, long time.

Actually, Molly was getting used to it.

Aunt Marie was very good to her and her friends, and it was fun talking at night when the lights were out.

Auntie Ree bought the girls ice cream sodas, and then they started home.

"We'll think of something else," said Mary Beth when they parted. "There are other fish in the sea."

When Molly went in the house, she saw something that lifted her spirits. It was a letter from Kyle!

She ran to her room and opened it.

"Dear Molly," it said. "I am writing back real fast because I don't think you should find a husband for your aunt. My mom says she likes being single again. And maybe your aunt Marie does too. Divorce is hard at first. But your aunt can have a house without having a husband."

Molly had not thought about that before. Her pen pal should know. Kyle's own mother was divorced! That made her an expert. And she had a house without a husband!

Kyle told her how she and her mother used to cry a lot. Then she went on in the letter about the new indoor skating rink in Golden Grove, and the new library. She signed her letter, "Lots of love, your pen pal Kyle."

Then there was a P.S. "Lots of parents argue a lot and don't get a divorce. I think you should ask your mom what's up. If they are getting one, they should tell you."

Molly couldn't ask her mom directly. Or could she? At least then she would know. Whether it was yes or no, she would know.

Molly put the letter down. She ran down the steps two at a time. Her aunt was washing her hair and her mother was alone in the living room, letting the hem down in Molly's skirt.

"Can I talk to you?" said Molly.

"Of course," said her mother.

"Are you and Daddy getting a divorce?"

Her mother looked surprised. "Of course not!" she said.

"Really?" said Molly. "But you were fighting last week."

Mrs. Duff frowned. "We weren't exactly fighting," she said. "Everyone has disagreements sometimes. Anyway, a fight doesn't mean divorce. And if we were, we would tell you. It wouldn't be your fault, you know."

There was to be no divorce! Molly's little family was going to stay as it was!

Suddenly Molly frowned. This meant that her dad would not have a house on the ocean. She would not go to California to visit him. She would not eat off little trays high in the sky.

Oh, well, it was a small price to pay to keep her family together. And she might be able to go to California some day anyway. To see Kyle.

The phone rang. Her aunt answered it. She talked quite a while and when she hung up, she came into the living room with wet hair, and a smile on her face.

"Guess what?" she said. "I got an apartment of my own! Only six blocks away!"

CHAPTER 11
Badge Day!

Molly couldn't believe her ears! Kyle was very, very smart! She had just told her that her aunt could have a house without a husband, and bang, she had one! Well, an apartment anyway.

She wondered if her aunt had ESP and Kyle's magic brain waves traveled over the miles to her. Or maybe her aunt knew all along she didn't need a husband to have a home.

"Why, Marie, there's no rush to leave!"

said Mrs. Duff, putting her arms around her sister.

Yes, there is, thought Molly. Even though Molly loved Auntie Ree, she wanted her room back.

"It's time," said Auntie Ree. "It's time for me to be on my own. You three really helped me through a hard time."

Auntie Ree and Molly's mother had tears in their eyes and hugged each other. Then they hugged Molly. Tears made Molly nervous because she thought they were sad. But sometimes tears were happy, she found out. It was hard to know which were which.

That evening they all trooped over to the new apartment, and Aunt Marie showed them where she planned to put everything and the pullout cot where Molly would sleep if she stayed overnight. She showed them the view of the pond from the kitchen window and the little fold-up ironing board that came out of the wall. The living room even had built-in bookcases for Auntie Ree's books.

"I'm so pleased for you!" said Mrs. Duff.

"It's a great place," said Mr. Duff. "And if you need any pictures hung or squeaky doors oiled, I'm your man!"

"Thanks," said Aunt Marie, laughing. "But I think I can handle it."

Molly couldn't wait to see Mary Beth. The next morning, she ran over to her house.

"My aunt is moving out!" she told her.

"Is she getting married?" asked Mary Beth.

Molly shook her head. "She doesn't want a husband!" said Molly. "She wants an apartment!"

Mary Beth looked doubtful. "Everyone wants a husband," she said. "My mom said so."

Molly usually believed what Mary Beth's mother said. But not this time. She was surprised to discover that adults could have different ideas about things and they could both be right.

Molly wrote a long letter back to her pen pal. She wrote it with red ink. She had to use a big envelope because there was so much news to tell her.

The next Tuesday at Pee Wee Scouts, Mrs. Peters said, "Let's hear all about your pen pals!"

Tim had a big package. "My pen pal sent me a baseball!" he said.

He tossed it to Kenny.

"Wow," said Tracy. "He's sure lucky."

More hands were in the air to tell about their new friends. Everyone's but Rachel's. Molly noticed that Rachel was very quiet. Rachel usually had a lot to say. Especially about her pen pal, Heather.

"Shari and I both baby-sit our little brothers," said Mary Beth. "We both want a lot of kids when we grow up."

"Mrs. Peters," said Ashley, "if Jason's

dad has to come here on business, Jason is going to come along and we'll go horseback riding together!"

"How nice," said Mrs. Peters. "This is just what I hoped would happen! You would have a new friend and get to meet!"

"I probably won't meet my pen pal," said Roger.

"Why not?" asked Kevin.

"Because I never wrote to her!" said Roger. "I think it's dumb!"

"You knew she wouldn't write back," scoffed Ashley. "You're afraid of rejection."

"My mom says we shouldn't close ourselves off from new experiences," said Patty. "I think that's what Roger is doing."

"My pen pal has the same name I do!" said Jody. "Just his first name," he added. "He collects CDs too."

"Is he handicapped?" asked Lisa.

Jody shook his head.

"Just because he collects CDs like Jody

and has the same name, doesn't mean he has a wheelchair!" said Tracy. "My pen pal has crutches but it's because she broke her leg climbing a tree." Then Tracy showed the sealing wax her mom had given her. "I melt a little and stamp my initial on it." She showed them the *T*.

One by one everyone told something about their pen pals.

"I'm glad you are enjoying writing letters," said their leader. "And I'm glad you are keeping an open mind and learning new things from them."

Molly raised her hand. "I learned from Kyle that even if your parents argue, it doesn't mean they will get a divorce."

As soon as she said that, Rachel burst into tears. Everyone was so surprised that no one said a thing. Finally Rachel wiped her eyes and said, "My mom and dad might get a divorce! Maybe I won't have anywhere to live!" Then she burst into tears again.

Rat's knees! All these days Molly had self-
ishly worried about her own aunt and her
own parents divorcing! And all the time it
was Rachel's parents who were having
problems! She never thought that anything

would happen in Rachel's happy family! Rachel's father was a dentist! Dentists did not leave their wives!

Mrs. Peters tried to comfort Rachel. So did Mrs. Stone. But Rachel put her head down on the table and would not look up. Molly didn't remember Rachel ever feeling bad, unless she was mad at Roger.

While Mrs. Stone was passing out the cupcakes, Molly went over and sat by Rachel. She put her arm around her shoulders.

"I'm sorry about your parents," she told her. "But my pen pal, Kyle, has parents who live apart, and it isn't too bad. They both love her, and she has two homes instead of one. And my aunt is divorced and she's real happy. Everyone doesn't have to be married to have a happy home."

Rachel did not look up.

"Anyway, maybe they won't get a divorce at all," said Molly. "Do you know for sure? I thought my mom and dad were, because they fought, but they didn't. Maybe you should talk to your mom and you'd feel better. And I'll give you Kyle's address if you want to write to her."

Molly gave Rachel a hug and went back to her chair. Mrs. Peters asked Rachel if she'd like to have her mother or father come and get her. Rachel shook her head. She wanted to stay.

Mrs. Peters looked sad, but she said, "Maybe these badges will cheer us up a little. I'm sorry to say that Roger will not get one today, but just as soon as he writes his letter and mails it, he will get his badge."

Everyone looked at Roger. This was the first time a Pee Wee Scout had not gotten a badge with the others! Sometimes they did not do much work for it, but they did something. But Roger hadn't done anything! He couldn't get a badge when he didn't even try!

Mrs. Peters passed out the pen pal

badges. Molly hoped Rachel's would cheer her up. They had a pen on them, and a little bottle of ink.

"Hey, what's this?" said Sonny, pointing to the pen and ink.

"It's a pen you write with, dummy," said Tracy.

"It doesn't look like my pen," scoffed Sonny.

"It's an old-fashioned pen people used to dip in ink," said Mrs. Stone. Molly pinned her badge on her blouse. It looked wonderful!

The Pee Wees sang their song and said their pledge. They didn't talk about good deeds. Today was badge day.

After the meeting, on the way out, Rachel came up to Molly.

"Thanks for telling me about your aunt," she said. "And Kyle's parents. But I hope mine don't get a divorce."

"I do too!" said Molly warmly.

"I'm going to talk to my mom about it," she said, wiping her eyes.

On the way home, Molly and Mary Beth sang the Pee Wee song all over again.

On Saturday Auntie Ree moved out. Mr. Duff rented a truck and helped his sister-in-law load it up.

They loaded the exercise equipment from the basement.

And all the bottles and jars and panty hose from Molly's room.

They packed her clothes, which were in Molly's closet.

Molly felt a little bit sad to see her aunt go. But she knew she could see her often. It was like having a new friend! And she had her own little room back, without having to have Roger for a cousin! It was a good thing that plan of Mary Beth's never worked out!

At the new apartment, Molly and her

mother and some of Aunt Marie's friends from work washed windows and waxed floors and moved clothes into the closet.

"Isn't it wonderful!" said Auntie Ree, after the last picture was hung on the wall.

Everyone agreed it was a cozy apartment.

"Come and see me soon!" said Auntie Ree to Molly. She gave her a hug. "You've been a super duper Pee Wee to me, Molly," she said, squeezing Molly again.

"I'll come on Tuesday, after Scouts," said Molly. "Can I bring my suitcase and stay overnight?"

"You bet," said Auntie Ree. "If your mom and dad say it's okay."

They did.

"But don't bring Skippy," Auntie Ree said with a laugh. "No dogs allowed in this building!"

A week later, Molly was walking home from her aunt's. When she passed Roger's

house, he dashed out, waving something in
his hand.

"I got it," he called to her. "I got my
badge."

"Did you cheat?" asked Molly.

"Of course not," said Roger. "I sent her a picture of myself holding that great big fish I caught last summer. And one of me flying a jet plane."

"You never flew a plane," said Molly.

"I did at the fair," said Roger. "It didn't go up in the air, but she doesn't have to know that."

He ran back in the house waving his badge.

Roger is hopeless, thought Molly. The only thing worse than having him for a cousin would be having him for a brother!

When Molly got home, she went to her room. It looked big and bare now, and she stretched out on her bed and enjoyed how quiet it was. The only sound was the hum of her little clock.

Then the phone rang. It was Rachel.

"My mom and dad are going to a marriage counselor," she said.

"What good news," said Molly. She knew

that Rachel's parents might still get divorced, but at least they were talking to each other and trying to figure things out. She felt very happy for Rachel.

"And I got a nice letter from Kyle. It really helped me feel a little better," said Rachel.

"Thanks for letting me write to her," she added shyly.

When Rachel hung up, Molly got a piece of her perfumed stationery and wrote, "Dear Kyle, it was really nice of you to write to Rachel. We all got our pen pal badges, even Roger. My aunt moved out last week. She has a nice place with a bed for me. It's nice to have my room back."

Molly wrote a few more lines and then wrote, "Love, Molly."

She addressed an envelope and put a stamp on it.

All the things she worried about were over.

Her aunt was happy.

Her parents were not getting a divorce.

She had a new friend, and a new badge.

And she had helped Rachel.

That was what being Pee Wees was all about.

Helping others.

She couldn't help Roger, but someday she might.

She wouldn't give up.

Rat's knees, it was great to be a Pee Wee—a super duper Pee Wee!

A LETTER FROM JUDY DELTON

Dear Pee Wee Readers,

If you like to write letters, maybe you could have a pen pal too. Perhaps your class in school could write to children in another city. Or you could write to someone you met on vacation, or a cousin or relative in another part of the country. Ask your parents to suggest someone.

If you want to collect stamps like some of the Pee Wees did, you can make your own album out of a photo album with plastic pages. Or you could keep your stamps in a small box or buy a regular stamp collector's album at a hobby store.

Watch for unusual stamps on the mail that comes to your house. When the

envelopes are thrown away, take the
stamps off first. If they won't come off,
you can soak them face down in a tray
of water to loosen them. When they're
dry, press them under some heavy books
to flatten them out.

See how many unusual stamps you
can collect. Exchange stamps with your

friends. Watch for stamps from other countries and ask your friends and relatives to save them for you.

Happy writing and collecting!
Love,
Judy Delton

LISA AND TRACY'S
CROSSWORD PUZZLE

Lisa and Tracy made this crossword puzzle. Lisa did the "across" clues, and Tracy did the "down" clues. Can you fill in the blanks? Answers on the next page.

LISA'S CLUES

Across:

1. A quiet Pee Wee.
4. Rachel took _____ dancing lessons.
5. Initials on Roger's shirt.
6. What Molly used to knit a sweater.
7. Rat's _____!
8. Mrs. Peters drives a _____.
9. Mrs. Peters's baby.
13. *Pee Wees on* _____. (title)
14. In book #1, the Pee Wees went to an _____ rink.
15. How old Molly is.
16. Jody gets around in a wheel_____.
17. One of these equals mushy stuff.
18. Molly's "fish," from *All Dads on Deck*.

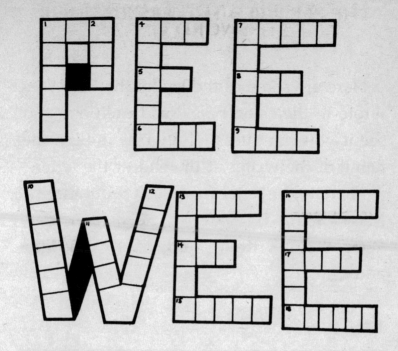

TRACY'S CLUES

Down:

1. A Pee Wee who has allergies.
2. Mary Beth's initials.
4. Sonny's pet (in *Peanut Butter Pilgrims*).
7. Molly wants to marry him.
10. Newest Pee Wee.
11. A Pee Wee on wheels.
12. The four-footed Pee Wee mascot. Arf!
13. *Blue* _____, *French Fries.* (title)
16. What the Pee Wees bake in book #1.

THE PEE WEES' LETTERS TO THEIR PEN PALS

Here are some of the letters the Pee Wees wrote to their pen pals. Read each one and see if you can guess who wrote it. Sign the name of the writer at the end of the letter.

There is one letter from each Scout: Molly, Mary Beth, Tracy, Lisa, Rachel, Ashley, Patty, Kenny, Kevin, Jody, Sonny, Roger, and Tim.

1

Dear Pen Pal,

I'm just a temporary Pee Wee Scout. I really live in California and belong to Saddle Scouts because I like horses and I like to ride. We have fun in Troop 23 too. My family travels a lot. I hope you write back.

Love, Ashley

2

Dear Pen Pal,

I'm only writing this because we have to, to get our badge. I hate to write letters. I hate to indent. It's dumb. My hobby is collecting lightbulbs.

Yours truly, _____ Tim

3

Dear Pen Pal,

How are you? I am fine. I am in Troop 23. My mother is assistant Scout leader. She serves the cupcakes. I have a brother and a sister and they are twins and they came on a plane. Please write back or I won't get my badge.

Sincerely, _____ Joanna

4

Dear Pen Pal,

I love to write letters. Do you? Even though you are a boy, I hope we can be pen pals. Some boys are nice but there is one boy in our troop who isn't. I have lots of badges, and lots of friends. Once my dad lost his job but he has an-other one now. My aunt got a divorce. She is staying at our house, sharing my room with me. It is crowded. I have no brothers and sisters, but I have a dog named Skippy. Please write back.

Love, _Molly_

5

Dear Pen Pal,

I am an only child. Are you? My dad is a den-tist. I take tap dance lessons. I like to shop for new clothes. I have another pen pal in Germany. I am going to go there and meet her some day. Do you like to travel? Do you take dance lessons, or any other lessons?

Sincerely, _Rachel_

6

Dear Pen Pal,

I have allergies. Do you have any? My hobby is crossword puzzles. My aunt gives me puzzle books. What are your hobbies? _Lisa_

Please write back, _____

7

Dear Pen Pal,

I collect CDs because I like music and I like to have parties at my house. I like being in Troop 23. The kids are nice. I am handicapped and have a wheelchair. My friend Molly likes to ride in my chair. She wants a wheelchair of her own but her mom said no. Please write back and tell me about yourself and your hobbies and stuff.

Love, _Jody_

8

Dear Pen Pal,

Do you like politics? I do. I want to be mayor when I grow up. Then maybe president. My girlfriend is Molly Duff. I gave her a pretty valentine once. Do you have any girlfriends? Well, I've got to go.

Love, _Kevin_

9

Dear Pen Pal,

Hi. How are you? Are you African American? It's okay if you aren't. I am the only African American kid in Troop 23. I don't have a dad. Neither does Tim Noon.

We have fun in scouts. We go skiing and skating and we used to sell doughnuts. I hope I get to meet you.

Love, _Tancy_

10

Dear Pen Pal,

Hi, I'm a twin. My brother is Kenny. It's fun being twins sometimes. But sometimes it isn't. You don't get to be alone much because twins are in the same grade and the same room and they are always at your birthday party. You have to share everything, even when you don't want to.

Let me know if you are a twin.

Love, _Patty_

11

Dear Pen Pal,

I have a big family. Lots of brothers and sisters. Some of them are married already. I have nieces and nephews. And aunts and uncles. I baby-sit a lot.

Troop 23 is lots of fun. Molly Duff is my best friend in it. On Halloween we came as a Popsicle and our legs were the sticks. Write back.

Love, *Marybeth*

12

Dear Pen Pal,

Hi. I am in Troop 23. My friends are Kevin and Jody and sometimes Roger. I have a twin sister named Patty. We make lots of stuff in scouts, like when we recycled, one girl made a wedding dress out of an old curtain and another one made a jewelry box out of an egg carton. I made something but I don't remember what.

Yours truly, *Kenny*

Dear Pen Pal,

I have to write to you even though you are a girl. Mrs. Peters said so. She said people are people. But I'll bet I can run faster than you. I am stronger than any one else in the Pee Wees. How many pounds of weights can you lift? Let me know. I live with my dad. Who do you live with?

Sincerely, _Roger_

Answers

Answers: 1. Ashley Baker 2. Tim Noon 3. Sonny Betz Stone 4. Molly Duff 5. Rachel Meyers 6. Tracy Barnes 7. Jody George 8. Kevin Moe 9. Lisa Ronning 10. Patty Baker 11. Mary Beth Kelly 12. Kenny Baker 13. Roger White.

ROGER'S RIDDLES

Why was Cinderella bad at soccer?
Because she ran away from the ball.

Why else was she bad at soccer?
Her coach was a pumpkin.

Why did they choose Snow White to be a judge?
Because she was the fairest of them all.

Why can't you catch a plane?
Because your arms aren't long enough.

What crime happens in a baseball game?
Hit and run.

What can't you eat for breakfast?
Lunch and dinner.

What did the monster eat after he had his tooth filled?
The dentist.

What would you do if a hippo sat in front of you in a theater?
Miss most of the movie.

Why do witches ride broomsticks?
Vacuum cleaner cords are too short.

What did Bobby catch when he went ice fishing?
A cold.

Who is the grave digger's girlfriend?
Whoever he can dig up.

Why did the lobster keep all the butter for himself?
Because he was shellfish.

What's Barbie's favorite party?
Barbie-cue.

Why is it hot in an empty ballpark?
Because there are no fans.

Can a turkey ever be a ghost?
No, but it can be a-gobblin'.

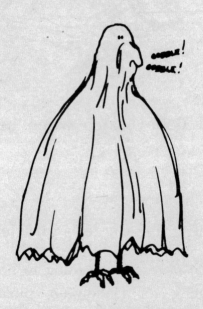

FAMOUS PEE WEE RECIPES

Whenever you bake, have an adult help you use the stove.

Every Tuesday the Pee Wees meet in Mrs. Peters's basement, and every Tuesday the Pee Wees look forward to Sonny's mother coming downstairs with a big plate of cupcakes. It is always a surprise to see what will be on the top of them!

Mrs. Peters's Cupcakes

Buy a box of chocolate fudge cake mix.

Follow the directions on the box.

When the batter is mixed, add $1/2$ cup of walnuts or pecans.

Add $1/2$ cup of drained maraschino cherries.

Add $1/4$ cup of chocolate chips.

Pour into fluted paper cups set in muffin tins.

Bake according to the directions on the cake box.

When cool, decorate according to holiday. (Orange frosting for Halloween, pink icing for Easter, green for Christmas, a cherry on top for Washington's birthday—think of more fun toppings yourself.)

Mary Beth's mother has a big family and has to bake often to keep the cookie jar filled. The cookies she makes most often are:

Mrs. Kelly's Peanut Butter Chocolate Cookies
Mix 1 cup chunky peanut butter, 1 egg, a 16-ounce can fudge frosting (saving out $1/3$ cup for icing the cookies), and $1^1/2$ cups flour. Shape into small balls, flatten, and bake for 7 minutes at 375 degrees. Cool and frost.

Ashley says the food in California is better than any food anywhere. One of the things she likes best is this pie. (Molly's grandma said the key limes are really from Florida, not California, but no one told Ashley this.) And it is a very good pie.

Ashley's California Key Lime Pie
Mix a 14-ounce can sweetened condensed milk, 2 beaten eggs, and 3 ounces key lime juice (ask for it at the supermarket). Pour into prepared gra-

ham cracker crust and bake for 10 minutes at 350 degrees.

Rachel worries a lot about eating healthy things. So she eats a lot of salads, which her mother says are very good for her.

Rachel's Pasta

Sauté 1 chopped onion, 1 minced clove of garlic, $1/2$ cup walnuts, and 10 ounces fresh washed spinach. Add 1 package cooked, drained pasta to this mixture and serve hot.

Sonny's Favorite Food

"It's jelly doughnuts, and you go to the bakery downtown and buy them. They are real gooey and sticky and get red raspberry jelly all over your face."

Thanks, Sonny.

Roger's father taught him to make this, to use up all the leftovers in the refrigerator, but Roger said he made it up himself. It is fast and easy, and you can eat it on the way to somewhere else because it goes between two slices of bread.

Roger's Sandwich

Stir-fry in a little olive oil whatever is in the refrigerator, like celery, asparagus, onions, chicken, carrots, spinach, garlic, pea pods, peas, pork, etc. (First cut everything into little pieces.) Then add one egg or two depending on how much is in the pan, swish it around with a spatula, add some cheese, and put it between slices of bread with a little ketchup on it.

When the Pee Wees go to Lisa's after school, there is usually some chocolate mousse in the refrigerator. Her mom makes it when company comes unexpectedly because it is so easy. And she makes it for Lisa because Lisa is a chocolate lover.

Lisa's Chocolate Mousse

Whip a pint of whipping cream until it is stiff, and fold in 3 tablespoons of real cocoa and 1 cup of hot fudge topping (cold) from a jar. Serve in pretty goblets.

Enjoy!